AF408031

SNOWBOUND WITH THE BOY NEXT DOOR

Young Adult Romance

Part Two

LIA LUCAS

Ardent Artist Books

Snowbound with the Boy Next Door - Part Two
Copyright © 2024 by Lia Lucas
All rights reserved.

Book Cover and formatting provided by Trisha Fuentes
https://bit.ly/m/trishafuentes

No part of this book may be reproduced in any form or by any electronic or mechanical means, including information storage and retrieval systems, without written permission from the author, except for the use of brief quotations in a book review.

ISBN: 979-8-3302-5558-0 (Paperback)

**Published by
Ardent Artist Books**
www.ardentartistbooks.com

About Ardent Artist Books

Ardent Artist Books was established in 2008.

We publish modern and historical romances once a month!

Get Your Free List: Published & Upcoming Books visit our website at:

https://ardentartistbooks.com/free-downloads

FREE DOWNLOAD
Updated Monthly!

Follow us on YouTube to see what new stories are on the horizon!

https://www.youtube.com/theardentartist

Like, Subscribe & Comment

❄

LET'S CONNECT!

Fuel your love of fiction with exclusive content and captivating insights from Ardent Artist Books. Whether you crave the thrill of modern narratives or the timeless elegance of historical fiction, our newsletter delivers a curated selection straight to your inbox.

Plus, as a welcome gift, receive a FREE downloadable eBook:

"The Family Fix"

https://mailchi.mp/567874a61a56/aab-landing-page

Contents

Chapter One

Maddie Sullivan's boots sank into the snow with each labored step, the once-familiar Crystal Lake campground now a treacherous white void. The wind howled, a furious beast intent on pushing her off course.

"Come on, Maddie," she muttered through chattering teeth. "You've got this. Just like the survival guides said."

But those guides hadn't prepared her for this. The blizzard intensified, snowflakes stinging her face like tiny needles. Maddie squinted, struggling to see more than a few feet ahead.

I should have listened to Mom about the weather forecast, she thought, regret gnawing at her insides. *Now I might freeze to death because I wanted to prove I could handle myself.*

A particularly strong gust nearly knocked her off her feet. Maddie stumbled, her hands plunging into the icy snow. The cold bit through her gloves, numbing her fingers instantly.

"No," she growled, forcing herself back up. "I won't give up. I can't."

Her legs trembled with exhaustion, each step a monumental effort. The pines that usually comforted her now loomed ominously, their branches weighted with snow, creaking in the wind.

Just as despair threatened to overwhelm her, Maddie's eyes caught a flicker in the distance. *A light?* Her heart raced, hope surging through her veins.

"Please be real," she whispered, blinking furiously to clear her vision.

The light remained, a beacon in the swirling white. Maddie's resolve hardened. She had a goal now, a lifeline to cling to.

With renewed determination, she pressed forward. The wind seemed to fight her every move, as if testing her will to survive. But Maddie was nothing if not stubborn.

"You won't beat me," she said to the storm, her voice barely audible above the howling gale. "I'm Maddie Sullivan, and I don't quit."

She thought of her family, probably frantic with worry. Of Brooke, her best friend who'd begged her not to go on this solo hike. And inexplicably, of Dexter Matthews, his easy smile flashing in her mind.

No, Maddie decided. *I'm not done yet. There are too many things left unsaid, too many adventures still to have. I'm only sixteen for crying out loud!*

Step by agonizing step, she inched closer to the light. It grew stronger, more defined. *A window, perhaps? Shelter, at last.*

Maddie's legs screamed in protest, but she ignored the pain. The light was her only chance, and she'd be damned if she'd let it slip away.

"Almost there," she encouraged herself. "Just a little further."

The storm raged on, unrelenting in its fury. But Maddie Sullivan trudged onward, her eyes fixed on that distant glow, determination etched into every line of her face.

Maddie's heart leapt as the shadowy outline of a cabin finally emerged from the whiteout. Her relief was so palpable she could taste it, sharp and sweet on her tongue.

"Thank God," she whispered, her voice hoarse and trembling.

As she stumbled the last few feet to the porch, her legs gave out. Maddie caught herself on the railing, her frozen fingers barely able to grip the rough wood. She stood there for a moment, panting, her whole body shaking violently.

"Come on, Maddie," she muttered. "You didn't come this far to freeze on the doorstep."

With a monumental effort, she hauled herself up the creaking steps. The door loomed before her, a barrier between life and death. Maddie reached for the handle, praying it wasn't locked.

The knob turned.

She almost wept with relief as she pushed the door open, practically falling into the dark interior. The wind howled at her back, driving icy fingers of snow into the cabin before she managed to slam the door shut.

Silence fell, broken only by Maddie's ragged breathing.

"Hello?" she called out, her voice echoing in the emptiness. "Is anyone here?"

No answer came. Maddie fumbled for her phone, using its feeble light to survey her surroundings. The cabin was small, rustic, clearly abandoned for some time. Dust motes danced in the beam of her light, and the musty smell of disuse filled her nostrils.

"Okay," Maddie said to herself, trying to steady her nerves. "You're safe now. Think. *Someone* started the fire. Someone obviously *lives* here."

She surveyed her surroundings. There was a table and two chairs in the corner by a kitchenette. A rug took over most of the wooden floor and some blankets were stacked up in the corner.

Maddie wasn't scared anymore, even though she was still tired. She knew she needed to get warm and dry and see what supplies she had left. As she went inside the dwelling, she started thinking about what to do next, even though a tiny voice inside her worried that this place might be a little creepy being all alone in the storm ... but someone started the fire.

Maddie pushed the thought away. She was alive, and that was what mattered. Everything else could wait.

As Maddie's eyes adjusted to the dim light, a sudden movement in the corner startled her. Her heart leaped into her throat.

Dex stepped in through the rear door. Firewood and kindling in his arms.

"Maddie?" He said, dropping the wood next to the hearth. "Thank goodness you're safe … I looked for you."

Maddie's heart turned over. *He did?* Maddie's practical nature quickly reasserted itself. "We need to take stock of our supplies," she said, pushing aside the flutter in her stomach at Dex's presence. "This storm isn't letting up anytime soon."

She began to move around the cabin, her eyes scanning for anything useful. "Look for blankets, matches, anything we can use to stay warm and dry."

Dex nodded, his usual carefree demeanor sobering slightly. "On it, boss."

As they searched, Maddie's thoughts whirled. *How long would they be stuck here? Did anyone know where they were? And how was she going to handle being alone with her secret crush in such close quarters?*

"Found some candles and a flashlight," Dex called out, interrupting her spiraling thoughts.

Maddie nodded, grateful for the distraction. "Good. I've got some canned food and water bottles in my backpack. We should be okay for a day or two, at least."

She tried to ignore the way her heart raced when Dex smiled at her, instead focusing on their immediate needs. *Survival first,* she reminded herself. *Everything else could wait.*

Maddie watched as Dex sauntered across the cabin, whistling a cheerful tune. Her eyes narrowed, frustration bubbling up inside her.

"How can you be so... so nonchalant about this?" she blurted out, her voice tinged with exasperation.

Dex turned, his blue eyes twinkling with mischief. "Come on, Maddie. Where's your sense of adventure? It's like we're in our own little snow globe!"

She huffed, crossing her arms. "This isn't a game, Dex. We're stranded in a blizzard!"

He chuckled, plopping down on a worn armchair. "I know, I know. But panicking won't help, will it?"

Maddie bit her lip, torn between admiration for his optimism and frustration at his apparent lack of concern. She busied herself arranging their meager supplies, trying to ignore the way her heart fluttered when Dex's gaze lingered on her.

"Hey," he said softly, his tone more serious. "We're in this together, okay?"

She looked up, meeting his eyes. Despite herself, Maddie felt a wave of comfort wash over her. "Yeah," she replied, offering a small smile. "I guess we are."

As the wind howled outside, they huddled closer to the fireplace, the shared warmth of the cabin drawing them together despite their differences.

The flickering candlelight cast dancing shadows on the cabin walls as Maddie and Dex sat cross-legged on the worn wooden floor. Between them lay a battered Monopoly board, its faded properties a stark contrast to the high-stakes game of survival they were playing in real life.

"Your turn," Dex said, tossing the dice to Maddie with a playful grin.

She caught them, her fingers brushing against his for a fleeting moment. A jolt of electricity shot through her, and she quickly averted her gaze. "Right," she muttered, rolling the dice.

As the game progressed, Maddie found herself relaxing, her guard slowly lowering. She even caught herself laughing at Dex's ridiculous attempts to haggle for Boardwalk.

"Come on," he pleaded, his blue eyes wide with mock desperation. "I'll throw in Mediterranean Avenue and my undying gratitude!"

Maddie snorted. "Nice try, Matthews. Your gratitude won't pay my rent when you land on my hotel."

Dex clutched his chest dramatically. "You wound me, Sullivan. I thought we were friends!"

"Friends don't let friends win at Monopoly," she retorted, surprising herself with the easy banter.

As the night wore on, they abandoned the game in favor of swapping stories. Maddie found herself sharing memories of her family's camping trips, her voice soft with nostalgia.

"I remember this one time," she said, a smile playing on her lips, "when I was seven. Dad tried to teach me how to fish, but I was so excited I fell right into the lake!"

Dex's laughter filled the cabin, warm and genuine. "I can just picture little Maddie, soaking wet and probably still trying to catch a fish!"

She chuckled, shaking her head. "You're not far off. I was determined to prove I could do it."

As Dex launched into a story about his own childhood misadventures, Maddie felt a strange mix of emotions swirling inside her. She watched him, illuminated by the soft candlelight, his animated gestures and bright smile captivating her attention.

"What?" Dex asked, catching her staring.

Maddie blinked, heat rushing to her cheeks. "Nothing," she mumbled, tucking a strand of hair behind her ear. "Just... thanks for keeping my mind off things, I guess."

He smiled softly, and Maddie's heart skipped a beat. "Anytime, Maddie. That's what friends are for, right?"

Friends. The word echoed in her mind, bringing with it a confusing blend of comfort and disappointment. Maddie pushed the feeling aside, reminding herself to focus on their situation. But as the night wore on, she couldn't help but wonder if there might be something more beneath the surface of their newfound camaraderie.

Dex leaned back, his eyes twinkling with mischief. "You know, I bet we could turn this whole situation into an epic adventure story. Picture it: *'The Daring Duo of Crystal Lake, Battling Blizzards and Boredom!'*"

Maddie rolled her eyes, but couldn't suppress a smile. "Only you could find the bright side of being stranded in a snowstorm, Dex."

"Hey, gotta keep our spirits up, right?" He winked, reaching for a dusty pack of cards on a nearby shelf. "How about a game of Go Fish? I promise not to push you into any imaginary lakes."

As they played, Maddie found herself torn between appreciating Dex's lighthearted attitude and worrying about their predicament. The wind howled outside, rattling the cabin's windows.

"Dex," she said hesitantly, laying down her cards. "Don't you think we should be... I don't know, planning something? What if the storm doesn't let up soon?"

He paused, his carefree expression faltering for a moment. "We've got shelter, warmth, and each other. That's a pretty good start, I'd say."

Maddie bit her lip, unconvinced. "But our families must be worried sick. And what if we run out of supplies?"

Dex reached across the table, gently squeezing her hand. "Hey, we'll figure it out, okay? One step at a time."

His touch sent a jolt through her, but Maddie couldn't

shake the nagging doubt. *Did he really understand how serious this was? Or was his optimism just a mask for fear?*

The cabin creaked ominously, and Maddie shivered. She stood, moving to peer out the frosted window. The world outside was a swirling white void, beautiful and terrifying.

"We need to be prepared," she murmured, more to herself than to Dex. "We can't just sit here and hope for the best."

Behind her, she heard Dex sigh. "Maddie, I get it. You're worried. But wearing ourselves out with worst-case scenarios won't help anyone."

She turned, meeting his gaze. For a moment, she saw a flicker of something – *concern? Fear?* – beneath his usual confident demeanor. It was oddly comforting to know he wasn't as unaffected as he seemed.

"You're right," Maddie admitted, her resolve strengthening. "But we can be positive and prepared. Let's inventory our supplies, okay? That way, we'll know exactly where we stand."

Dex nodded, a small smile playing at his lips. "There's the Maddie I know. Always with a plan."

As they began sorting through the cabin's meager provisions, Maddie felt a renewed sense of purpose. *They'd get through this,* she told herself. *They had to.*

Chapter Two

A FEW HOURS LATER

Maddie's heart raced as she peered out the frost-covered window, the world beyond a swirling vortex of white.

"I can't see anything out there," she said, her voice barely audible over the storm's fury.

Dex moved beside her, his breath forming small clouds in the frigid air. "At least we made it inside. This place is like an ice box though."

Maddie nodded, rubbing her arms for warmth. The cold seeped into her bones, making her shiver uncontrollably. She couldn't help but think of the warm campfire they'd left behind, now surely extinguished by the blizzard's onslaught.

"We need to get the fire going again," Dex said, already moving towards the stone fireplace.

Maddie watched as he expertly arranged kindling and logs, struck a match, and coaxed a small flame to life. The fire crackled and popped, casting flickering shadows across the cabin's rustic interior.

As the warmth slowly began to spread, Maddie and Dex huddled close to the hearth, their shoulders touching. Maddie's pragmatic side warred with the flutter in her chest at Dex's proximity. She'd never been this close to him before, not even during their shared classes at Sequoia Grove High.

"Here," Dex said, draping a scratchy wool blanket over their shoulders. "This should help."

"Thanks," Maddie murmured, pulling the blanket tighter around herself.

The wind rattled the cabin's windows, a stark reminder of the danger lurking just beyond the wooden walls. Maddie's thoughts drifted to her family, hoping they were safe in their RV at the campsite.

"Do you think the storm will let up soon?" she asked, more to break the silence than anything else.

Dex shrugged, his usual carefree demeanor somewhat subdued. "Hard to say. But hey, at least we're not stuck out there, right?"

Maddie nodded, grateful for his optimism even as worry gnawed at her insides. She stared into the dancing flames, mesmerized by their hypnotic movement. The fire's warmth slowly thawed her frozen limbs, but a chill of uncertainty remained.

"I've never seen a storm like this before," she admitted softly.

"Me neither," Dex replied. "But we'll get through it."

Maddie turned to look at him, caught off guard by the earnestness in his blue eyes. For a moment, she saw past his easygoing exterior to the strength that lay beneath. It was oddly comforting.

"Yeah," she said, managing a small smile. "I guess."

Dex shifted, his shoulders tensing as he cleared his throat. The crackling fire filled the silence for a moment before he spoke, his voice uncharacteristically hesitant.

"Maddie, I... there's something I need to tell you."

Maddie's heart skipped a beat. She turned to face him, eyebrows raised in curiosity. "What is it?"

Dex ran a hand through his tousled blonde hair, a nervous gesture she'd never seen from him before. "I've... I've had a crush on you for a while now. At school, I've wanted to talk to you, to ask you out, but I never knew how."

The confession hung in the air, heavy as the storm clouds outside. Maddie's eyes widened, her mind reeling. *Dex? The carefree, charming quarterback had feelings for her?*

"You... what?" she stammered, struggling to process this new information.

Dex's blue eyes met hers, vulnerability shining in their depths. "I know it might seem out of the blue, but it's true."

Maddie's brow furrowed, her pragmatic nature kicking in as she tried to reconcile this revelation with the Dex she thought she knew. The boy who always seemed so confident, so at ease with everyone. *How could he have been harboring these feelings?* "I thought you had a crush on my bestie Brooke … all boys crush on Brooke."

"Brooke?" He shook his head, "Nah, I mean, she's hot and all, but I … like you."

Maddie held the blanket around her shoulders closer.

"But... why didn't you say anything before?" she asked, her voice barely above a whisper.

Dex let out a self-deprecating chuckle. "Believe it or not, you kind of intimidate me, Maddie Sullivan. I was afraid you'd think I was just another dumb jock."

Maddie's mind raced, replaying every interaction they'd had at Sequoia Grove High. *Had there been signs she'd missed? Moments of connection she'd overlooked?*

As the storm raged on outside, Maddie found herself facing a different kind of tempest within.

Maddie took a deep breath, her hazel eyes searching Dex's face. "I... I never thought you'd see me that way," she admitted, her voice softening. "You always seemed so confident, so sure of yourself."

Dex's lips quirked into a lopsided smile. "Guess we both had the wrong idea about each other, huh?"

A chuckle escaped Maddie's lips, surprising her. "I suppose so." She paused, gathering her courage. "To be honest, I have a crush on you too."

Their eyes lock and hold.

Maddie wanted to kiss Dex.

Dex wanted to kiss Maddie.

But…

"Even in a raging snowstorm?" Dex teased, gesturing to the cabin window.

"Especially then," Maddie replied, glad of the diversion.

Dex's eyes lit up. "Speaking of finding joy, want to hear about the time I got stuck in a tree during my first camping trip?"

Maddie leaned in, intrigued. "You? Stuck in a tree?"

As Dex launched into his tale, complete with animated gestures and comical voices, Maddie found herself laughing harder than she had in years. The storm outside faded into the background as they swapped stories, from Maddie's disastrous attempt at making s'mores to Dex's infamous canoe capsizing incident.

"I can't believe you fell into Crystal Lake trying to impress Sarah Jenkins," Maddie giggled, wiping tears from her eyes.

Dex clutched his chest in mock offense. "Hey, I'll have you know I looked very graceful flailing about in the water."

Their laughter mingled in the air, creating a warmth that rivaled the fire's glow. As their mirth subsided, Maddie realized something had shifted between them. The walls she'd carefully constructed were crumbling, revealing a connection she'd never expected to find.

The cabin cradled them in a cocoon of warmth, a stark contrast to the howling tempest beyond its walls. Maddie snuggled deeper into the plush blanket draped over her shoulders, inhaling the comforting scent of pine and woodsmoke. The crackling fire cast dancing shadows across the room, its golden light softening the rough-hewn logs.

"This is... nice," Maddie murmured, her eyes drawn to the mesmerizing flames.

Dex nodded, his profile illuminated by the firelight. "It's like we're in our own little world."

As Maddie watched him, a flutter of something unfamiliar stirred in her chest. She quickly averted her gaze, her pragmatic mind wrestling with these new, confusing emotions.

"You okay?" Dex asked, concern evident in his voice.

Maddie forced a smile. "Yeah, just... thinking."

But her thoughts were a tumultuous whirlwind. *This was Dex – the most popular, JV quarterback, Dex. So why did her heart race when he smiled at her? Why did his laughter make her feel warm all over?*

"Penny for your thoughts?" Dex prodded gently.

Maddie bit her lip, conflicted. "I don't know, Dex. This is all happening so fast. I'm not sure..."

"Not sure about what?"

She sighed, struggling to articulate her fears. "About... this. Us. What if we're just caught up in the moment? What if, when we get back to school, everything changes?"

Dex reached out, hesitantly taking her hand. "Maybe it will. But maybe that's not such a bad thing."

Maddie's practical side screamed caution, but her heart... her heart whispered of possibilities.

Maddie's heart raced as she met Dex's earnest gaze. "What do you enjoy about being the quarterback?" she asked, her voice barely above a whisper.

Dex's eyes lit up. "I've always loved football," he confessed. "Traveling to other schools, competing against other like-minded players, like me."

A gust of wind rattled the cabin windows, making Maddie jump. She took a deep breath, steadying herself.

"That sounds exciting," she replied. "I tried out for cheerleading."

"Yeah? That's amazing," Dex said, genuine admiration in his voice. "What happened?"

Maddie smiled, warmth blooming in her chest. "Didn't make the JV squad," she admitted. "My splits weren't split enough."

Dex squeezed her hand. "I'm sure you were good. I heard it's hard to make that squad. Just like football, it's tough to make the team."

She hesitated, then whispered, "I just hate failing. Letting people down."

"I get that," Dex nodded. "But you know what? I think you're braver than you realize."

Outside, the storm howled, a crescendo of wind and ice. Snow piled against the windows, obscuring the world beyond. Maddie shivered, despite the warmth of the fire.

"Listen to that," she murmured. "It's like the storm is trying to swallow us whole."

Dex's thumb traced circles on her palm. "But we're safe in here. Together."

Maddie's breath caught in her throat. She looked at Dex, really looked at him, seeing past the carefree exterior to the depth beneath.

Dex's eyes sparkled with mischief, a grin spreading across his face. "You know what? We should make a game out of this."

Maddie raised an eyebrow. "A game? We're trapped in a cabin during a blizzard, Dex."

"Exactly!" He jumped up, his enthusiasm infectious. "Let's see who can come up with the most outrageous silver lining to our situation. I'll start: we're getting an exclusive preview of the next ice age!"

Despite herself, Maddie couldn't help but laugh. "You're ridiculous."

"Come on, Maddie," Dex encouraged. "Give it a shot. What's the bright side here?"

She hesitated, then said, "Um... we're getting really good at building fires?"

"That's the spirit!" Dex cheered. "Though I think we can do better. How about: we're living out our very own survival romance novel?"

Maddie's cheeks flushed. "Dex!"

He held up his hands, laughing. "Hey, I'm just calling it like I see it."

As their laughter subsided, a comfortable silence fell between them. Maddie found herself studying Dex's profile, illuminated by the flickering firelight. *How had she never noticed the gentle curve of his jaw, the way his eyes crinkled when he smiled?*

"You know," Dex said softly, turning to meet her gaze, "I meant what I said earlier. About admiring you."

Maddie's heart skipped a beat. "I... I'm starting to see you differently too," she admitted.

Dex reached out, his fingers brushing a stray lock of hair from her face. The touch sent a shiver down her spine that had nothing to do with the cold.

Chapter Three

Maddie tucked a stray lock of brown hair behind her ear, the flicker of candlelight casting shadows on her face. "Did I ever tell you about the time I tried to build a treehouse with my brother?" she asked, a laugh bubbling up from her throat.

"Build? No, you didn't," Dex replied, his eyes lighting up with curiosity as he leaned in closer. The wind outside banged against the cabin walls, but it felt distant, like an echo from another world.

"We were ambitious but clueless. It ended up being this lopsided platform wedged between two branches," Maddie recounted, her hazel eyes sparkling with the vivid memory. "It was our little sanctuary until it collapsed under the weight of our dog."

"Wait—your dog?" Dex chuckled, the sound rich and warm in the confined space.

"Yep, a seventy-pound golden retriever who thought he was a lapdog." She smiled at the absurdity of it all. "Your turn. Any escapades?"

"Plenty," Dex admitted, his blonde hair catching the light as he raked a hand through it. "But there's one that stands out. I once convinced Ava to go on a 'treasure hunt' I made up on the spot." His blue eyes danced with mischief. "We dug up half the backyard looking for a time capsule that didn't exist."

"Your sister must've been thrilled," Maddie mused, picturing the scene and the dirt-streaked faces that would have accompanied such an adventure.

"Let's just say we found a different kind of treasure." Dex's grin was contagious, pulling a laugh from Maddie that mingled with his.

The gusting storm seemed to howl in protest at their mirth, a reminder of the world beyond their bubble of warmth. Maddie glanced around the rustic interior of the cabin, seeking a distraction from the relentless wind.

"Hey, how about another round of Monopoly?" Maddie pulled out the weathered box, the corners frayed and the color faded. "I haven't played this in like, forever—I forgot how fun it was."

"Neither have I," Dex said, taking the game from her hands. Their fingers brushed briefly, sending an unexpected jolt up Maddie's arm. "Let's see if I'm as good a mogul as I was last time."

"May the best baron win," Dex teased, unfolding the board between them. The candlelight cast tall, wavering shadows across the colorful squares, turning their game into a dance of light and darkness.

"Or baroness," Maddie countered, a playful spark in her eyes.

"Indeed," Dex agreed, his smile softening as he met her gaze. "Baroness Sullivan, let the games begin."

Maddie unfolded the board with delicate care, placing it on the small wooden table that leaned slightly to one side. The flickering candlelight cast an inviting glow over the board's pastel properties and the duo settled on either side, the warmth pushing back the chill from the storm outside. Dex reached for the silver game pieces, his fingers grazing Maddie's as they both sought the top hat.

"Oops, sorry—seems we both have a thing for classic style," he chuckled, retracting his hand for her to take it.

"Classic indeed, but I think I'll let you have the honor of the top hat, Mr. Monopoly," Maddie replied, a smirk playing on her lips as she instead selected the little dog. His laughter mingled with hers, light and unburdened, filling the cabin with a mirthful resonance.

"Alright then, Baroness Sullivan," Dex said, rolling the dice with a flourish, "prepare to have your empire crumble before you."

"Is that so?" Maddie retorted, tilting her head slightly, her hazel eyes alight with challenge. "We'll just see about that, won't we?"

As the game continued, their playful competitiveness took center stage. With each roll of the dice, they leaned in closer, the world narrowing to the squares of property and paper money between them. Maddie found herself captivated by the way Dex's eyes lit up with every successful transaction, his boyish grin infectious. She discovered a strategic thinker behind his easygoing charm, a side of him she'd never seen at Sequoia Grove High.

"Ah, Pacific Avenue, a personal favorite. You planning on

building a hotel there?" Maddie asked, watching as Dex contemplated his next move.

"Maybe," he admitted with a sly smile. "But then again, I might just surprise you."

"Surprises are good," she agreed, feeling a flutter in her stomach. "Keeps life interesting."

Their conversation flowed as they traded properties and navigated through the intricacies of the game. Maddie shared her tactic of always going for the railroads—solid and dependable investments, much like how she approached her camping trips: prepared for anything. Dex listened intently, nodding along and sharing his own strategy of risk for the possibility of greater reward, much like his decision to play quarterback.

The storm outside seemed to fade from their awareness, reduced to a distant murmur compared to the vibrant reality of their shared experience. They were no longer two teenagers from neighboring campsites; they were fellow moguls, vying for control of their cardboard domain.

"Looks like you've got quite the collection of properties there," Dex observed, gesturing at Maddie's steadily growing estate. "But don't think for a second I'm not plotting my comeback."

"Plot away," Maddie responded, the corners of her mouth lifting in amusement. "I welcome the challenge."

Maddie stretched across the Monopoly board, her fingers inching towards the dice. With a flick of the wrist, they rolled, clattering against the cardboard. But as she withdrew her arm in anticipation, her sleeve brushed the candle. In slow motion, it teetered, and then with an almost silent protest, succumbed to gravity. The flame sputtered out, leaving them wrapped in sudden darkness.

"Oops," Maddie whispered, her voice swallowed by the pitch-black room.

A beat of silence hung between them, heavy with the weight of the unexpected blackout. Then, as if on cue, their tension broke and laughter erupted, echoing off the cabin walls. It was pure and unrestrained, the kind that bubbles up from deep within—a release of pent-up nerves and suppressed giggles.

"Adventure finds us even in board games, huh?" Dex's voice danced through the darkness, closer now. Maddie could feel his warmth nearby, a comforting presence in the void.

"Seems like it," Maddie replied, still chuckling. She fumbled around for the candle, her hands brushing against the cool surface of the table and the scattered game pieces.

"Here, let me." Dex's hand met hers in the dark, and together they righted the candle. A match struck, flaring bright before settling into a steady glow. Shadows leaped to life around the room, playing over their faces as the light restored visibility.

"By candlelight then," Dex suggested, the soft light casting a golden hue across his features. "Makes it more... I don't know, dramatic?"

"Cozy, I'd say." Maddie nodded, feeling a sense of warmth that had little to do with the candle. She resettled herself, the familiar shapes of the game coming back into focus.

The storm outside seemed to fade again, its fury muffled by the thick wooden walls. Inside this little haven, the world narrowed to the flicker of candlelight and the shared space of play. They leaned forward, their elbows nearly touching, and Maddie felt a spark of something electric—more thrilling than any bolt of lightning.

"Your turn, Madison," Dex said with a mischievous glint in his eyes, passing her the dice.

"Thanks, Dex." Maddie's fingers closed over the cool plastic, a small smile playing on her lips.

As they continued their game, each roll of the dice seemed to weave them closer, binding them in a tapestry of playful competition and quiet companionship. The sounds of their voices filled the cabin, a symphony of laughter and lighthearted jabs at one another's expense.

"Bankrupt already?" Maddie teased as Dex handed over his last few bills.

"Only strategically bankrupt. You wait, I'll make a grand comeback," he promised with a grin that was all confidence and charm.

"Strategy or wishful thinking?" she quipped, raising an eyebrow in mock skepticism.

"Bit of both," he conceded, and she laughed, delighting in the banter that came so easily between them.

"Ever think about what's next? After high school, I mean," Maddie asked, tucking a strand of brown hair behind her ear as she collected rent from Dex's unfortunate landing.

Dex leaned back, his gaze drifting to the ceiling before meeting hers. "I want to travel. See everything—every corner of the world." His voice was a soft rumble, filled with longing. "What about you?"

"College, probably," she replied, but her hazel eyes were distant, lost in thoughts unspoken. "But sometimes, I dream of writing stories. Stories that could take someone on adventures, even if they're stuck in one place."

"Like a storm-bound cabin?" Dex's tease was gentle, pulling a small smile onto Maddie's lips.

"Exactly like this," she admitted, feeling an unexpected warmth bloom in her chest.

Their conversation meandered, touching on fears of the unknown, the pressures of expectations, and the hidden excitement for future freedoms. With each revelation, a layer of their defenses crumbled, leaving raw honesty in its place.

The wind's wail crescendoed, a relentless assault against the fragile barrier between them and the tempest outside. Maddie glanced towards the window, watching as snowflakes battered the glass, each flake a tiny dancer in the night's wild ballet.

"Sounds angry, doesn't it?" Dex's observation pulled her attention back to the room, its coziness a stark contrast to the chaos beyond.

"Do you think they're looking for us?" Maddie murmured, her voice barely above the storm.

"No," Dex admitted, "Visibility is probably at zero right now, it's dark out now, and the storm hasn't let up."

"My dad once told me there was a girl who got lost from her party, and the rangers looked for her for days," Maddie let out, holding the blanket closer to her body.

"What happened to her?" Dex asked, curious.

"They found her three days later," Maddie admitted, "She found a shelter in a cave and ate the candy bars she stole away in her backpack."

As if in agreement, the cabin shuddered, a particularly vicious gust finding its way through the cracks. Instinctively, Maddie moved closer to Dex, their shoulders touching. The simple contact felt like an anchor in the turbulence, a silent promise of solidarity.

"Scary how something so beautiful can turn so fierce," she said, her breath visible in the chill air that had started to seep in.

"Isn't that the truth," Dex replied, wrapping an arm around her. The gesture was protective, his touch steady and reassuring.

They huddled together, two figures cast in the dance of candlelight and shadow. Each blast of wind, each creak of the timbers, drew them nearer, until their sides pressed flush, a single unit braving the storm. There was strength in their unity, comfort in the shared beat of their hearts.

"Think we'll make it through the night?" Maddie half-joked, though her grip on his hand betrayed her apprehension.

"Of course we will," Dex answered, his voice low and sincere.

A surge of gratitude washed over Maddie, and she rested her head against Dex's shoulder. Maddie's gaze lingered on Dex, tracing the contours of his face highlighted by the erratic dance of candlelight. His eyes, deep blue pools in the flickering shadows, held a glint of something that made her pulse quicken—recognition, perhaps, or the dawning of something new and terrifyingly wonderful. Her heart, once a metronome of practicality, now skipped erratically with emotions she couldn't have planned for.

"Thank you," she whispered, the words carrying more weight than their syllables suggested. Gratitude for his presence, for his warmth, for the way he saw her—not just as Maddie Sullivan from Sequoia Grove High, but as someone worth holding onto amidst the chaos of a storm.

Dex's hand found hers, a comforting pressure against her skin. "For what?" His voice was a soft rumble, like distant thunder rolling over the lake outside.

"For being here. For...this." She gestured vaguely between them, unable to articulate the tangle of feelings that connected them.

He smiled, a crooked expression that sent shivers down her spine. "Trust me, it's mutual."

They sat there, entwined, while the tempest raged on outside—a sharp contrast to the gentle sanctuary they had built within the wooden walls of the cabin. The silence between them was filled with unspoken words, promises that hung in the air, delicate as the snowflakes sticking to the windowpanes.

With their shoulders touching, Dex leaned over and grazed his lips across Maddie's. It was a sweet kiss, a tender one, filled with affection and reassurance. "We'll be OK."

As the night stretched on, weariness crept into their bones, the adrenaline of shared confessions ebbing away. They moved apart almost reluctantly, each settling into their makeshift beds on opposite sides of the room. The space between them was filled with flickers of candlelight and the soft sounds of the cabin breathing around them.

In the quiet, Maddie pulled the blanket tighter around her shoulders, watching as Dex mirrored her actions. Their eyes met across the dim room, a silent conversation passing between them. In that look, there was an acknowledgment of the day's emotional odyssey, a mutual understanding of the strength they had given one another—a strength that would outlast the longest of nights.

"Goodnight, Maddie," Dex called softly, his voice a lullaby against the howling wind.

"Goodnight, Dex," she replied, her eyelids growing heavy with the promise of sleep.

Maddie lay cocooned in the warmth of her sleeping bag, the last vestiges of candlelight casting dancing shadows across her closed eyelids. She turned on her side, facing where Dex rested, his breaths rhythmically whispering through the charged silence. The blizzard's roar dimmed to a distant whisper, its icy fingers unable to pierce the gentle haven they had woven together.

Maddie was so glad that her story did not include unprotected sex … because that's where they were heading. A confined cabin, a boy, a girl equals sex. *Isn't that what happens in the romance books she's read?* Not *her* romance with Dex … and she was glad for it. For not having been placed in that situation. Her first time will be with him someday, she thought as she felt herself fall asleep. *Not just tonight.*

In sleep, Maddie's face softened, the lines of cautious pragmatism smoothed by dreams tinted with hope. Her chest rose and fell in a steady cadence, mirroring the pines outside that swayed but did not break. Even in repose, there was a resilience about her, an enduring strength that promised she would weather any storm—real or metaphorical.

Dex, sprawled across his own makeshift bed, was a picture of carefree slumber. The tension that earlier marked his features now dissolved into peace, his athletic form relaxed. One arm flung above his head as if reaching for dreams just beyond his grasp, he seemed every inch the adventurer, undaunted even in the land of sleep.

Chapter Four

THE NEXT AFTERNOON

Maddie's fingers brushed over the radio, its static hum a stark reminder of their isolation. The broadcaster's warning about avalanches hung in the air, as cold and present as the snow outside. "Dex," she said, her voice cutting through the silence, "we need to plan our route carefully. We can't risk getting caught in an avalanche."

Dex nodded, his eyes reflecting the seriousness of her words. They huddled together over the worn map spread across the wooden floor, tracing possible paths with their fingertips. Each line they drew skirted around the mountains' shoulders like cautious whispers, avoiding the steep inclines where snow lay heavy and threatening.

"Safer routes will take longer," Dex observed, but there was no complaint in his tone—only the steady beat of determination.

"Longer is better than never," Maddie retorted, her gaze not leaving the map. They agreed on a path, one that zigzagged through the safer valleys, a dance between caution and the urgency tugging at their chests.

With the plan etched firmly in their minds, they turned their attention to gathering what few supplies remained. Maddie reached under her makeshift bed, pulling out a battered backpack. She opened it wide, its gaping mouth ready to swallow their survival essentials.

"Flashlight," Dex said, placing the item into the bag. Its beam would be their guide through the encroaching dusk.

"Compass," Maddie followed, securing the instrument next to the flashlight. It would serve as their anchor when the whiteout threatened to erase the world around them.

"First aid kit," they said together, a small smile flickering on Maddie's lips despite the gravity of their situation. The kit was tiny, but each bandage and antiseptic wipe was a pact against despair.

They took turns stuffing the backpack, their movements synchronized by shared resolve, each item a piece of hope they could cling to. The weight of the bag grew, heavy with more than just the necessities—it carried their will to persevere, to find their way back to everything they held dear.

"Think we've got everything?" Dex asked, zipping the backpack closed, his fingers lingering on the seams as if ensuring it could bear the burden.

"Everything we can carry," Maddie replied, slinging the pack over her shoulder, feeling the comforting tug against her back. It was an embrace, a silent acknowledgment of the journey ahead.

"Then let's look at the map again," Maddie suggested, unfurling the wrinkled paper on the wooden table they had used for meals that now seemed like a distant memory. The lines and contours stared back at them, a riddle of safety amidst danger.

"Okay," Dex nodded, leaning over her shoulder, his breath warm against her cheek. She fought the urge to lean into the comfort it offered. "The radio mentioned this ridge here," he pointed, "as a high-risk zone for avalanches."

"Right." Maddie traced the line with her finger, her mind picturing the ominous snowpack lurking above. "We need to skirt around it. Take the longer way through the valley."

"Longer but safer," Dex agreed, his blue eyes locking onto hers. In them, she saw the reflection of her own fears and the determination to overcome them.

"Exactly." Maddie marked their chosen path with a pencil, each stroke a silent vow to tread carefully. "We'll need to be cautious, watch for signs of shifting snow, listen for... you know."

"Cracks in the silence," Dex finished for her, understanding without needing words. Their shared experiences in the wilds had taught them much, but nothing quite like this test of endurance.

"Let's keep an eye out for any markers we can use too—landmarks, anything unusual that stands out. It could help us if visibility gets bad," Maddie said, rolling the map back up, its edges curling like the uncertain horizon beyond the cabin walls.

"Good thinking, Madison." Dex's use of her full name was rare, reserved for moments that bridged the gap between casual camaraderie and the depth of their connection.

"Ready?" She hesitated, feeling the weight of the decision pressing down upon them. This wasn't just leaving the cabin; it was stepping into the unknown, where every choice carried the weight of consequence.

"Ready as I'll ever be," Dex replied, shouldering his own pack—the one with the makeshift sled tied to it. His smile was brave, a shield against the encroaching cold.

Maddie took a deep breath, savoring the familiar scent of pine and firewood one last time before opening the door. They were about to leave the safety of the known for the treacherous embrace of the snow-covered wilderness. But they were not alone; they had each other.

"Wait!" She yelled, fumbling in the front pockets of her backpack.

Maddie's fingers trembled as they clutched the pen, the ink barely cooperating in the cold that seeped through the cabin walls. Beside her, Dex leaned over a scrap of paper torn from an old journal they had found among the cabin's sparse possessions. His brow furrowed with concentration as he scrawled out their intentions.

"If we're not back by nightfall," Maddie murmured, "they'll know where to start looking." Her words hung in the air, a silent prayer for safety and reunion.

"Let's just hope it's us finding them first," Dex said, his voice low but unwavering. He folded the note carefully, like it was a fragile promise they were leaving behind.

Together, they placed the note under a small, rustic tin cup on the table—a beacon amidst the quiet chaos. It was a tangible piece of hope that their families would return to find the cabin warm and welcoming once more.

With a last glance at the interior that had been their unexpected haven, Maddie shouldered her backpack. The weight of it felt grounding against her shoulders, a reminder of the purpose she carried.

"Okay, let's do this," she announced, her voice steady despite the fluttering in her chest.

The cabin door creaked open, surrendering them to the elements. A gust of wind snatched at their clothes, biting at any exposed skin with icy teeth. Snowflakes danced wildly in the air, a blizzard's ballet, disorienting and beautiful. They stepped out, and the door swung shut with a soft thud—a chapter closing behind them.

"Which way?" Dex asked, squinting into the white expanse.

"North-northwest," Maddie replied, consulting the compass with numb fingers. It wobbled precariously before settling, its magnetic needle a steadfast guide amidst the swirling snow.

"Lead the way, Madison," Dex said, a playful lilt in his voice that defied the grimness of their situation.

"Always," she shot back, a faint smile tugging at her lips. With a nod, they stepped forward, each print in the snow a declaration of their resolve. Their breaths materialized before them, whispers of warmth in the freezing air as they began their journey toward the unknown.

Maddie squinted against the relentless flurries, her boots plunging into the cold embrace of fresh snow. With each step, she carved a path for them, her legs aching with the effort. Behind her, the makeshift sled they had crafted scraped and hissed, announcing their progress through the silent world.

"Doing great, Madison," Dex's voice came from behind, encouragement wrapped in the warmth of his breath that puffed out in visible clouds.

"Thanks, Dex," she replied, not turning but feeling a swell of gratitude for his presence. She adjusted her grip on the rope tethered to the sled, her fingers stiff from the cold.

The terrain began to rise, sloping upward in a daunting stretch of white. They paused at the base, Maddie tilting her head back to gauge the incline. The slope loomed like a giant's slide, its surface untouched save for the patterns etched by the wind.

"Looks risky," Dex murmured, coming up beside her. His eyes scoured the expanse, searching for telltale signs of danger.

"Let's check for layers," Maddie suggested, her voice barely above a whisper as if speaking too loudly might disturb the precarious peace.

They dropped to their knees, digging at the snow. It yielded under their gloves, revealing a cross-section of what lay beneath. Compact layers sandwiched between looser ones—an ominous lasagna of instability.

"Could be worse," Maddie mused, trying to sound more confident than she felt. "But we should definitely take it slow."

"Agreed." Dex nodded, his expression sober. He stood, offering Maddie a hand which she took gratefully, the contact sending a surge of warmth through her. Together, they surveyed the ascent before them.

"Use the sled as an anchor," she instructed, brushing a rogue strand of brown hair from her eyes. "We can't afford any mistakes."

"Right behind you," Dex said, positioning the sled so that it dug into the snow, a makeshift barricade against the pull of gravity.

Maddie tested the ground before her, planting her feet firmly with each tentative advance. The snow compressed beneath her weight, holding firm. Dex echoed her movements, his gaze never leaving the path ahead.

"Steady," he reminded her, just as her foot slipped, sending a spray of snow skyward.

"Got it," Maddie responded, regaining her balance with a dancer's grace. Her heart hammered against her ribcage —a tiny drummer propelling her onward.

Step by cautious step, they ascended, the world narrowing to the space of their shared breaths and the crunch of their boots. Above them, the sky remained a gray canvas, indifferent to their struggle. Below, the campsite and cabin seemed part of another lifetime—one defined by laughter and the crackle of a campfire instead of the silence of survival.

"Almost there," Dex breathed as the slope gradually eased, their summit within reach.

"Almost," Maddie echoed, allowing herself a moment to believe in the possibility of safety, the chance of finding their families.

The sharp report of fracturing ice shattered the silence, a thunderous warning that ricocheted through the valley. Maddie's muscles tensed, her breath hitching in her chest as she whipped her head around. A plume of white billowed from a slope nearby, snow tumbling and roaring like a wild beast unleashed.

"Move!" Dex's voice cut through the tumult, sharper than the winter air.

Together, they lunged to the side, their makeshift sled clattering against the uneven ground. They huddled behind an outcrop of rock, the overhang providing scant protection against the roar of nature's fury. The avalanche was a smaller one, yet it sent a spray of snow dusting over them like a chilling caress.

"Are you okay?" Maddie's words came out in a puff of fog, her hazel eyes wide and searching as she turned to Dex.

"Yeah," he replied, his own breath ragged, blue eyes reflecting the stark terror of the moment.

They waited, hearts pounding in tandem until the rumble faded into an oppressive silence. As the snow settled, Maddie felt the tremble in her hands subside, her practicality reasserting itself with forceful clarity.

"We'll have to reroute," she said, her voice steady despite the adrenaline that still coursed through her veins. "We can't risk another slide."

"Agreed," Dex nodded, brushing a flurry of snowflakes from his blond hair. His usual carefree demeanor had been replaced by a focused intensity.

Maddie pulled out the map they'd crafted earlier, her fingers tracing along the dotted lines and symbols that represented safety and danger. With each pass, she reassured herself of their path, the pragmatic part of her mind calculating angles and distances with precision.

"Let's give the slopes a wide berth," she suggested, pointing to a narrow valley that snaked between two imposing peaks.

"Looks solid," Dex concurred, squinting at the route. "Longer, but safer."

"Sometimes the long way is the only way," Maddie murmured, more to herself than to Dex. She tucked the map back into her pocket, its edges crinkling like the leaves back home in the fall.

They set off once more, their steps measured and deliberate. The snow seemed less of an adversary now, more a canvas upon which they charted their survival. Dex took up the rear, pushing the sled, his encouragement now a silent presence that Maddie felt at her back. Maddie's legs burned with every step, her breaths coming in icy puffs that disappeared into the frigid air. A glance at Dex showed his face set in grim determination, his blonde hair dusted with a frosting of snowflakes. The world around them had shrunk to an expanse of white, broken only by the stark silhouettes of trees standing sentinel over their arduous journey.

"Let's stop for a bit," she gasped, her voice a ghost in the wind.

Dex nodded, relief evident in the slump of his shoulders as they found a relatively sheltered spot beneath an evergreen whose boughs sagged under the weight of the snow. They sank onto the makeshift sled, the repurposed door now a sanctuary from the relentless cold. Maddie pulled out a crinkling packet of trail mix, the nuts and dried fruits a treasure trove against the gnawing hunger.

"Here," she offered, pouring some into his cupped hands.

"Thanks, Madison." Dex popped a raisin into his mouth, the nickname slipping out, a reminder of school halls and simpler times.

The snack was meager, but each chew released a burst of much-needed energy. They leaned against each other, sharing body heat, their breath mingling in the space between them. For a fleeting moment, the howl of the wind seemed softer, the chill less biting.

A comfortable silence settled over them, filled with shared remembrances and unspoken emotions. In their huddle for survival, the barriers between them seemed to crumble, replaced by a trust as solid as the earth beneath the blanket of snow.

Maddie noticed the way Dex's arm tightened around her, protective and sure. She rested her head against his shoulder, allowing herself this moment of respite, this sliver of peace amidst the chaos. Her heart drummed a rhythm that spoke of more than just friendship, but the confession remained locked behind her lips, a secret yet to bloom.

"Ready to keep going?" Dex's voice broke the spell, though his reluctance mirrored her own.

"Always," she replied, her hazel eyes capturing the last rays of the sun before it dipped below the horizon, taking with it the day's fears and leaving behind the promise of tomorrow.

Together, they rose, muscles protesting but spirits unyielded. They stepped back into the dance with nature, each print in the snow a testament to their journey—a journey of miles and of the heart, where every challenge faced and every obstacle overcome drew them closer, not just to safety, but to each other.

Chapter Five

"Keep close," shouted Dex against the roar of the storm, his voice barely cutting through the cacophony.

Maddie nodded, her hazel eyes squinting to discern his outline ahead. She hoisted her backpack higher onto her shoulders, its weight a constant reminder of the gravity of their situation. They were two figures, alone, pitted against nature's upheaval.

Their boots crunched in synchrony over the freshly laid blanket of snow, muffled thuds marking their progress. They moved with deliberate care, knowing that haste could spell disaster. Each step was a silent question posed to the earth beneath—would it hold or betray them?

"Watch your step," Dex cautioned as they approached an uneven patch where the snow had drifted into deceptive softness.

"Got it," Maddie replied, her voice steady despite the lump of anxiety lodged in her throat. She followed Dex's footprints, his athletic frame navigating the terrain with a confidence she admired. Maddie matched his pace, unwilling to let the distance between them grow.

The blizzard seemed to mock their resolve, intensifying as if to test their tenacity. They leaned into the wind, two saplings bent but unbroken amidst the tempest's fury. Even the campsite's familiar landmarks were shrouded in obscurity, the once welcoming expanse now a labyrinth of shadows and drifts.

"Can you see anything?" Maddie called out, her words almost swallowed by the storm.

"Nothing yet," he yelled back, his silhouette a blur against the relentless white. "But we'll get there, just keep moving."

Maddie drew a deep breath, her lungs stinging from the frigid air. The scent of pine, once so invigorating, was now a ghostly presence beneath the onslaught of winter's breath. Step by cautious step, she followed Dex, each one a testament to the trust she placed in him, a trust that grew with every shared hardship.

Together, they pressed on, carving a path through the chaos, their journey a dance of survival choreographed by necessity. The cold seeped into their bones, a chilling reminder of the mountain's indifference to their plight, but still, they advanced—one step, then another—into the heart of the blinding storm.

Maddie's heartbeat thrummed in her ears, a staccato rhythm that matched the crunch of snow beneath their boots. Each gust of wind was a cold slap against her face, a reminder of nature's raw power. She watched Dex's broad shoulders cutting through the gale ahead of her, his steps sure and unfaltering, while her own feet dragged, heavy with doubt.

"Keep close," Dex called over his shoulder, his voice barely audible above the howl of the blizzard.

"I'm trying!" she shot back, her tone edged with the terror of being left behind in this white wasteland.

The world around them was reduced to mere shades of gray, the snowfall a relentless veil that threatened to erase their very existence. Maddie's thoughts churned like the storm: *Were they walking in circles? How much further could they endure?*

Just then, as if sensing the silent crescendo of her fears, Dex slowed, turning to face her. His eyes, those clear pools of blue, searched her face. Without a word, he reached out, his hand finding hers in the blind whiteness. The warmth of his touch jolted her, a spark of life in the frozen expanse.

"Hey," he said, his voice softer now, "we'll make it. Trust me."

His fingers tightened around hers, a lifeline thrown across the void of her uncertainty. A surge of something more than warmth coursed through her—a mix of gratitude, comfort, and an unspoken promise that no blizzard could chill the connection between them.

"Okay," she replied, squeezing back, allowing herself to lean on his strength, his optimism fueling her waning resolve.

They stood for a moment, two figures alone against the elements, bound by a shared determination. Then, with hands clasped and hearts bolstered, Maddie and Dex continued their journey into the tempest, each step a silent vow to face whatever lay ahead—together.

The incline rose before them, a silent challenge veiled in white. Maddie blinked away the icy tendrils that clung to her lashes and peered up at the daunting path ahead. Each breath formed a cloud of vapor that danced away into the blizzard, joining the whirling chaos.

"Looks like Mother Nature decided to build a wall," Dex quipped, his voice almost lost in the howling wind. He tested the snow's depth with his boot, probing for solidity.

"Or a mountain," Maddie added, trying to match his lightness despite the leaden feel of her limbs. Her muscles protested the idea of climbing, but there was no going around—only up.

Without another word, Dex began to ascend, cutting into the pristine surface with measured steps. His movements were fluid, each step purposeful, as he carved a narrow trail into the slope. Maddie watched, momentarily entranced by the rhythm of his progress, the snow yielding to his resolve.

"Stay close," he called over his shoulder, his figure half-swallowed by the flurry. "Step where I step."

"Right behind you," she replied, though her voice sounded small against the vastness of their snowy adversary. She focused on the imprints left by Dex's boots, placing her feet in the compacted indentations. The climb was slow, an exercise in persistence and trust.

Maddie felt her legs burn with effort, each step a testament to her fatigue. But she couldn't stop—not when every moment brought them closer to safety, to warmth, to the familiar faces that must be worrying over their absence. The thought of her family, gathered around the hearth at Crystal Lake Camp Ground, spurred her onward, their imagined relief a beacon in the gloom.

She dared a glance upward and saw Dex's back, strong and steady. His optimism seemed to seep from his very skin, a silent promise that they would not succumb to the cold, that despair would not claim them. It was a strange comfort, this reliance on someone who had been little more than a heartbeat in the night, a presence just out of reach.

Maddie summoned the image of her mother's gentle smile, her father's hearty laugh, and Brooke's infectious cheer. They were waiting, believing in her return. With each arduous step, Maddie reaffirmed her resolve. She would not let them down.

Her breaths became ragged, the air sharp as it filled her lungs. But Maddie pushed through, driven by an inner strength she hadn't known she possessed. The snow whispered secrets beneath their feet, tales of those who'd traversed these lands long before the campsite had borne witness to summer laughter.

"Keep moving, Madison," Dex encouraged without looking back, his tone warm against the frosty air. "We're doing great."

"Thanks," she managed, her words punctuated by the crunch of snow.

<h1 style="text-align:center">Chapter Six</h1>

The incline grew steeper, and with it, a gust of wind surged, as if the mountain itself were exhaling a frosty breath. Maddie squinted against the icy particles that peppered her face, each sting a reminder of the countless challenges they had already overcome. Dex's firm grip on her hand was the anchor she clung to, his presence a beacon in the whitewashed world that threatened to swallow them whole.

"Can't see much," she called out, her voice nearly snatched away by the wind.

"Trust me," Dex replied, his words barely audible over the howl of the storm.

She did. Implicitly. It wasn't just the warmth of his hand that gave her comfort, but also the steady rhythm of his pulse, an unspoken pledge that he would not let her falter.

A sudden crack, sharp as a gunshot, split the air, reverberating through their bodies. They halted, statues in a shifting landscape. The ground vibrated beneath their boots, a treacherous whisper that spread ice down Maddie's spine.

"Did you hear that?" Her question hung between them, a fragile thread in the chaos.

Dex's eyes met hers, the blue of his irises darkened by concern. "I heard it."

They stood on uncertainty made manifest, the ledge hidden under snow's deceitful blanket, its stability as fleeting as the shadows playing across Dex's face. The mountain seemed to hold its breath, waiting for their next move, as if it were a sentient being aware of the fragility of human life balanced upon its back.

"Careful," Dex murmured, his gaze locked onto the path ahead, searching for signs of solidity in a world that offered none.

Maddie's heart pounded, a drumbeat syncing with the tremor of the earth. There was no turning back, only forward, into the unknown that lay shrouded in white. And so, they stood still for a moment longer, two figures carved from hope and determination, bracing against the mountain's silent warning.

Adrenaline surged like wildfire through Maddie's veins, her pulse a rapid tattoo against the silence of the storm. Beside her, Dex's breath misted in the air, his eyes scanning the treacherous landscape for any sign of escape. They couldn't trust the ground that whimpered and groaned beneath their weight.

"Over there," Dex's voice cut through the howl of the wind, barely more than a whisper but filled with urgency. He pointed to their left where the mountain offered a narrow ridge, a jagged line against the chaos of white.

"Looks risky," Maddie replied, each word measured despite the tremble she could feel building within her.

"Risky is better than certain," he countered, his optimism an anchor in the storm.

She nodded, the motion small but resolute. Dex led the way, his steps cautious yet steady on the slender path carved into the mountainside. Maddie followed, her breathing shallow, her focus narrowed to the boots in front of her and the sureness of Dex's back. She concentrated on the crunch of snow underfoot, the only rhythm in this frozen world.

The ledge they had left behind groaned a warning, a reminder of the fragility of their situation. Maddie pushed the thought away, replacing it with the solidity of the ridge under her palms as she used her hands for balance. She let out a slow breath, trying to calm the fluttering in her chest, attempting to match Dex's confidence with each inch they progressed.

"Almost there, Maddie," Dex called back to her, his tone light, belying the gravity of their ascent. His casual courage was a lifeline thrown across the chasm of her fears.

"Right behind you," she managed to say, her voice steadier than she felt. The cold bit at her cheeks, the only visible part of her not wrapped in protective layers, but inside, warmth blossomed – not from exertion, but from something else, something unspoken that seemed to grow with every challenge they faced together.

They moved in harmony, two parts of a whole, their shared silence speaking volumes. The ridge, narrow as a tightrope, demanded all of Maddie's attention, each step a testament to the trust she placed in Dex, in herself, in the intangible thread that connected them.

The wind picked up, a feral creature howling its fury as Maddie and Dex inched along the narrow ridge. It clawed at their coats, tugged at their hats, and whispered threats that could send them tumbling with one false step. The air was a frozen blade against their skin, but they moved with a rhythm born of necessity, each foot placed with painstaking care.

"Keep moving," Dex grunted, his voice snatched away by the savage gusts. They couldn't afford to stop, not with the wind's icy fingers trying to pry them loose from their precarious path.

Maddie nodded, her focus laser-sharp on the space just ahead of her boots. She imagined herself as a mountain goat, sure-footed and unshakable, even as her heart hammered a frantic beat. The fear was there, a constant hum in her veins, but it was dwarfed by an ironclad resolve. Survival was the only option.

Finally, the ridge began to widen, and the ground underfoot shifted from treacherous to merely unwelcoming. With a few more steps, they emerged onto a plateau that promised respite. Maddie's lungs burned as she gulped down the frigid air, each breath crystallizing before her eyes.

"We made it," Dex said, his relief echoing hers. He turned to face her, and despite the layers of winter gear, she saw the strain etched into his features, a testament to the ordeal they'd endured.

Together, they paused, the world around them a panorama of white, the peaks standing like silent sentinels under a heavy sky. The beauty was stark, unforgiving, and utterly magnificent. For a fleeting moment, the danger they faced seemed to diminish, giving way to the splendor of the wilderness.

"Look at this place," Maddie whispered, her words a mix of awe and reverence.

"Nature's masterpiece," Dex replied, his gaze sweeping over the horizon. "But let's not give it a chance to finish us off."

A smile tugged at the corner of Maddie's mouth, the spark of humor a welcome warmth amidst the cold. They shared a nod, an unspoken agreement that they were far from done—that together, they would conquer whatever lay ahead. And with that, they stepped forward, leaving the treachery of the ridge behind and embracing the unknown challenges of the mountain.

Maddie's boots crunched over the freshly packed snow, each step a declaration of intent. Dex led the way, his silhouette a beacon of resolve against the swirling whiteness that threatened to swallow them whole. Her breath came in short bursts, visible puffs of life in the icy air, as her muscles protested the relentless pace.

"Almost there," Dex called back to her, his voice barely carrying over the relentless wind.

"Right behind you," she responded, though her voice seemed small and distant even to her own ears.

As they trudged on, Maddie found herself studying Dex —the way his shoulders squared against the blizzard, how he occasionally glanced back to ensure she was still there. In his eyes, a storm all their own raged—a tempest of fatigue wrestling with fierce determination. It dawned on her then, in the midst of nature's fury, that their journey was more than a battle against the elements; it was a testament to the unwavering spirit they shared.

Her heart, once thudding with trepidation, now drummed a rhythm of burgeoning hope. She realized that whatever doubts had clouded her mind were melting away like ice beneath a springtime sun. This boy, who laughed freely and dreamed boldly, had won her heart not by shielding her from the storm, but by facing it at her side.

"Madison," Dex said, his hand finding hers, "we've got this."

The touch sent a jolt through her, not unlike the thrill of watching lightning split the sky from the safety of her porch back home. There was strength in his grip, an unspoken pledge that echoed louder than any words could have.

"Always," she affirmed, squeezing his hand in return.

Their journey resumed, their clasped hands a lifeline amidst the chaos. With each careful step, their bond solidified, forged in the crucible of adversity. The mountain loomed ahead, its challenges insurmountable to some, yet to Maddie and Dex, it was merely another hill to climb together.

Dex's steady presence calmed the fluttering in Maddie's chest, his optimism a lighthouse guiding her through the fog of fear. Together, they were more than two high school sweethearts braving the elements; they were partners, equals in a dance with danger where trust was the music and love the steps.

And with that realization, Maddie knew that no storm could ever be too fierce, no night too dark, as long as they faced it united. The mountain, once a daunting foe, now stood as a witness to the enduring power of their love, a challenge not to defeat them but to define them.

Their path wound onward, through the relentless blizzard, towards the promise of tomorrow. And with each step, Maddie felt the truth of it all—their story was one of triumph, not tragedy; a tale of two hearts beating bravely against the odds.

Maddie's breath came out in short, visible puffs as they trudged onward, the snow beneath their feet compacting with a satisfying crunch. She kept her gaze fixed on Dex's broad back, the way his shoulders moved rhythmically with each step, a silent metronome against the dwindling fury of the blizzard. Each breath was a misty affirmation of life, each heartbeat a drum in the symphony of survival.

The wind, once a relentless force, now whispered apologies as it weaved through the trees, tugging gently at the loose strands of Maddie's hair. She blinked away the frost that clung to her lashes, and there it was—a sliver of blue amidst the grey, like hope piercing through doubt. Sunlight, shy and tentative, peeked through the dissipating clouds, casting a golden glow on the white expanse around them.

"Look," she breathed out, her voice a fragile thread in the vast tapestry of the wilderness.

Dex turned, his smile a slow spread of warmth on his chapped lips. "There's our silver lining," he said, the light catching in his eyes, turning them into clear pools of azure.

They stopped for just a moment, allowing themselves this brief respite from the relentless push forward. Maddie's fingers found Dex's, their hands fitting together like two pieces of a puzzle long separated. The touch sent a ripple of comfort through her, more potent than any fire could provide.

"Almost feels like the mountain is smiling down at us, doesn't it?" Dex mused, his thumb tracing circles over the back of her hand.

"Or maybe it's just relieved to see us go," Maddie replied, her lips curving to match his grin.

They shared a laugh, the sound carrying lightly on the breeze, mingling with the rustle of pine needles. It was a laugh of triumph, of shared secrets and memories forged in adversity. It was the laugh of two souls who had glimpsed the fragility of life and found something unbreakable within each other.

"Can we stop for a moment?" Maddie asked, searching for somewhere to sit.

"Yea—yeah, let's sit on that log over there," Dex agreed, pointing toward the area.

Chapter Seven

Maddie shifted on the weathered log, her gaze trailing over the sprawling view before her. The pine-scented air was a familiar comfort, a gentle nudge against the weight of thoughts she'd been carrying. Beside her, Dex tossed a small stone into the distance, his eyes following its arc with a quiet intensity that mirrored her own.

"Quite a trek, huh?" he said, breaking the stillness that had enveloped them. His voice was a warm thread in the cool tapestry.

She nodded, tucking a stray lock of brown hair behind her ear. "Never thought we'd make it past Dead Man's Cliff." A smile crept onto her lips, not quite reaching her hazel eyes. The memory of scaling the sheer rock face flickered across her mind—a testament to their resilience.

"Or that we'd find our way down after the map took a swim," Dex added, chuckling softly. His laughter was like sunlight piercing through clouds, and for a moment, Maddie allowed herself to bask in its glow.

Her smile widened, genuine this time. "We've come a long way from being the kids who couldn't even set up a tent."

"True. But hey, look at us now." Dex stretched out his arms as if embracing the world around them. "Survival experts."

"Or just lucky," Maddie countered, her pragmatic side surfacing. She glanced at him, noting the carefree way his blonde hair fell into his eyes. It was that optimism of his, that unyielding spirit, that drew her in.

"Maybe a bit of both," he conceded, his blue eyes locking with hers. There was a depth there, an understanding that seemed to bridge the gap between them.

The moment lingered, and Maddie felt something within her shift. It was as though the forest itself was urging her to open up, to share the part of herself she kept hidden behind practicality and caution. She took a deep breath, tasting the tang of pine on her tongue.

"I'm scared, you know," she admitted, her voice barely above a whisper. "Not of the cliffs or getting lost... but of what happens when this is all over. When we go back to reality."

Dex turned towards her, his expression softening. "I get that. I'm always chasing the next adventure, afraid of standing still. Afraid of missing out."

"Or missing someone," Maddie added, her heart thrumming in her chest.

"Exactly." Dex reached out, his fingers grazing hers, tentative yet certain. "But here, with you, I feel like I've found something worth stopping for."

"Me too." The words escaped Maddie before she could hold them back. They hung between them, fragile and bold all at once.

They sat in silence, the kind that speaks volumes, each lost in the swirl of fears, hopes, and dreams that had surfaced. In the quiet of the forest, with the lake reflecting the sky's endless possibilities, Maddie and Dex found a shared vulnerability that bound them closer than any adventure could.

A shadow crossed Dex's face. "I wish we could keep this... simplicity. Back home, everything's so complicated. Expectations, pressure..."

"Like football?" Maddie probed gently, sensing the unspoken weight on his shoulders.

"Yeah, football," he sighed. "Sometimes I wonder if I'm even playing for myself anymore."

"Because of your dad?" Maddie asked.

"No, not just him." Dex turned away, picking at the bark on the log. "It's everyone. The team, the school... you know how it is."

"Actually, I don't," Maddie said, feeling a sudden rift opening. "Not everyone expects you to be something you're not, Dex."

"Easy for you to say," Dex shot back, frustration edging his voice. "You've got it all figured out."

"Figured out?" Maddie's brow furrowed. "Just because I don't wear my doubts like a varsity jacket doesn't mean I don't have them."

Dex looked at her, his eyes searching hers. "Sorry, I didn't mean to——"

"Assume?" Maddie interjected, standing up from the log. "Yeah, you did."

Dex stood as well, facing her. "Maddie, I..." His words trailed off, the tension palpable.

"Look, we're different, I get it," Maddie relented, her voice softer now. "I plan, you leap. I worry, you soar."

"Maybe that's not such a bad thing," Dex offered, taking a tentative step closer.

"Maybe not," Maddie conceded, her heart rate settling as she met his gaze. "We balance each other out."

"Like a seesaw," Dex grinned, a spark of their earlier warmth returning.

"Exactly." Maddie's lips twitched into a smile. "A seesaw that sometimes tips too far one way."

"Then we just have to find our way back to the middle," Dex said, reaching out for her hand.

Maddie hesitated, then let her fingers intertwine with his. "Back to the middle," she echoed.

The sunlight filtered through the leaves, casting dappled patterns on the ground, as Dex and Maddie stood side by side.

Maddie released a breath she didn't know she'd been holding. The interplay of shadows and sunlight on the forest floor seemed to mirror the tumult of emotions within her.

"Look," Her voice was barely above a whisper, yet it sliced through the silence like a knife. She pointed up at the sky, "The clouds are breaking up."

Dex gazed up and smiled, "That's a good sign, Maddie."

"I know," she agreed, standing up off the log. "That means, the storm has stopped and they'll be gathering a search party."

"Exactly," Dex said, gathering his backpack. "Let's keep moving."

Dex turned toward her, his face open. "You good?"

"Yeah, let's go." She fidgeted with her own backpack and swung it over her shoulder. "Can I tell you something?"

Dex didn't look back at her who trailed behind him. "Sure, what?"

Maddie, looked down at her boots stomping in the snow. "It's just... sometimes I feel like there's this side of me that nobody gets to see." Maddie paused, her heartbeat drumming in her ears. "A side that dreams a little more... romantically than people would expect."

"Romantically?" Dex quickly turned around, his eyebrow quirked up, but his smile was gentle, not mocking.

Maddie nodded, hazel eyes flickering with vulnerability. "Yeah. And I guess I'm scared because... what if those dreams don't... what if they're just silly, or—"

"Or what if they're not?" Dex cut in, walking backward, facing her.

"Or what if they are, and... and I end up alone because of them?" Maddie's confession hung between them, delicate and fraught with the weight of unspoken hopes.

Dex halted and reached out, his hand brushing against hers—a touch that spoke volumes. "Maddie, look at me," he urged softly.

Reluctantly, she lifted her gaze to meet his ocean-deep eyes. "You're not going to end up alone. Your dreams matter. And for what it's worth, I think your romantic side is pretty amazing."

"Really?" A tentative smile began to form, but her eyes still held a glimmer of doubt.

"Really." Dex's tone left no room for argument. "And, uh... I've had dreams too. About someone who's been right here all along."

"Someone?" Maddie echoed, her pulse quickening, a fresh wave of hope surging through her.

"Someone strong, passionate about nature, and... who plans the best camping trips ever." Dex's grin was infectious, his words laced with sincerity.

"Sounds like quite a person," Maddie replied, her previous fears receding like shadows at dawn.

"More than you know," Dex said quietly, his hand now firmly holding hers. "And if she happened to have feelings for an optimistic, adventure-seeking jock, *well...* I'd say he's the luckiest dude around."

The air around them seemed to shimmer with possibility, each shared glance weaving the fabric of a future neither had dared to articulate until now. Their connection, once veiled in uncertainty, now sparkled with the clarity of mutual affection.

"Is that so?" Maddie's voice was steady, her heart daring to embrace the dream that felt suddenly within reach.

"Yeah... that's so," Dex confirmed, the softness in his eyes reflecting back her own yearning.

In the quiet cocoon of the forest, and amid the towering pines, Maddie felt the last of her reservations dissolve. For the first time, she allowed herself to fully believe in the promise of a 'we' shaped by shared dreams and bolstered by a bond that had weathered both doubts and disagreements.

"Thank you, Dex," she whispered, grateful for the understanding that only he could provide.

"Anytime, Madison." His use of her full name was a vow, a pledge of presence in whatever lay ahead.

Their hands remained entwined, a silent testament to the resilience of young love blooming against the backdrop of the wilds.

Still holding hands, Dex pulled Maddie ahead, "Let's keep going."

"Yes, sir," Maddie beamed, squeezing her hand in his.

And then Dex stopped.

He halted his trek in the middle of a clearing.

"Madison," he whispered, his breath tickling her ear, sending shivers down her spine. Her name, spoken with such tenderness, felt like a caress.

Her eyes found his, and in them, she saw the reflection of her own hopes, trepidation giving way to something bold and thrilling. The space between them crackled with anticipation, a silent symphony that crescendoed with each heartbeat.

He closed the distance, her eyelids fluttering shut. The moment their lips touched, it was as if time itself exhaled, a pause in the eternal rush. Soft and hesitant at first, the kiss deepened, a confluence of desire and affection that swelled like a wave cresting upon the shore.

Sensations bloomed across Maddie's skin—warmth where Dex held her close, the rough texture of his jacket under her fingertips, the sweet hint of marshmallow on his breath from the s'mores they'd shared earlier.

This kiss was a promise, a declaration penned in the language of touch and taste. It was the tender unraveling of every guarded secret, the melding of two souls that had danced around the precipice of love, now leaping into its depths.

Maddie's world had narrowed to the space between their parting lips, the lingering warmth a testament to what had just transpired. Dex inched back, his eyes a deep blue ocean of emotion that seemed to pull her in all over again. Her heart, a rapid drumbeat in her chest, matched the cadence of his.

"Wow," Dex breathed out, the single word hanging between them like a delicate secret. Maddie could only nod, her usual eloquence stolen by the moment.

"Did that just…?" Maddie's voice trailed off, her hazel eyes searching his for confirmation, for something solid to hold onto amid the whirling emotions.

"It did," Dex confirmed, his hand reaching out to gently tuck a stray lock of brown hair behind her ear. His touch was a spark, reigniting the embers of their connection, promising more.

"We should keep going," Maddie affirmed, freely reaching over and hugging him.

"Guess we're doing this, huh?" Dex said, his smile tentative but growing stronger with every second—he hugged her back.

"Seems like it," Maddie replied, her pragmatic nature yielding to the sweet chaos of young love. A laugh bubbled up from within her, surprising in its lightness. *I can't wait to tell Brooke!*

Chapter Eight

Even though the sun was beginning to peek through the clouds more, the wind wailed like a chorus of specters as Maddie pressed forward, her boots sinking deep into the snow with each labored step. The cold gnawed at her cheeks, turning them a rosy hue that belied the harshness of their situation. Beside her, Dex's breath came out in short puffs, visible plumes dissolving quickly in the frigid air.

"Keep moving," she murmured, more to herself than to Dex, though he nodded, his eyes squinting against the white that still surrounded them.

They trudged on, the world around them a blur of white and gray. Every muscle screamed in protest, but Maddie's resolve was an anchor in the snow; she would not let it sweep her away. Her thoughts drifted to the safe familiarity of Sequoia Grove High, where hallways echoed with locker slams and laughter, a stark contrast to the silent expanse that now enveloped her and Dex.

"See that?" Dex's voice cut through the veil of snow, sounding oddly calm despite the urgency that drove them.

Maddie followed his pointing glove to a break in the relentless white—a clearing ahead. It wasn't much, just an open space where the trees seemed to have conspired to give them a moment's respite, but it was enough. Enough to breathe, enough to think, enough to hope.

"Could be a sign," Dex said, his grin barely visible beneath his frost-laden scarf.

"Or a trap," Maddie countered, her pragmatism a shield against disappointment. Yet, she couldn't ignore the flutter in her chest, the same kind that whispered secrets under starlit skies by Crystal Lake Camp Ground.

"Only one way to find out," Dex replied, and they plunged into the promise of shelter, leaving behind the relentless pursuit of the storm.

As they crossed the threshold into the clearing, the world seemed to pause, granting them a momentary reprieve from their fight. Here, the snow lay untouched, a pristine canvas spread before them, the edges of the clearing framed by the stoic watch of pine trees.

"Look at this place," Dex breathed out, wonder lacing his words. Maddie's gaze followed his, taking in the serene beauty that defied the chaos they had left behind. "You could build a house here!"

"It's like a different world," she whispered back, allowing herself a sliver of awe. The snowflakes here fell with a gentle grace, as if respecting the sanctity of the hollow they had stumbled upon.

"Seems we're not the only ones looking for some peace," Dex said, tilting his head toward a pair of rabbits nestled against a fallen log, their fur a stark contrast to the snow.

"Let's not disturb them," Maddie replied softly, her heart warming at the sight. For a fleeting second, she saw a reflection of themselves in the small creatures—seeking solace, seeking survival.

"Agreed." Dex nodded, and together, they moved across the clearing with newfound respect for the stillness it offered.

Maddie's pulse quickened, a drumbeat syncing with the howl of the wind. Beside her, Dex's breath came in visible puffs, mirroring her own. They trudged forward, the snow a relentless adversary, when the silhouette of safety materialized through the flurry—a figure standing firm against nature's fury.

"Hello!" Dex called out, his voice a bright lance piercing the dull white around them.

The officer turned, and even at a distance, the authority etched into his stance cut through the chaos of the storm. He raised an arm, signaling them, his posture as sturdy as the mountains looming in the backdrop.

"Over here," Maddie's voice was barely above a whisper, but it didn't matter. Officer Mike Harrison had already spotted them, his eyes trained on their forms like a seasoned eagle on its quarry.

With each step closer to Officer Harrison, the crushing weight of the blizzard seemed to lift, replaced by a buoyant tide of relief. His presence was a lighthouse guiding them home. The snow underfoot felt less like a barrier and more like the final stretch of a marathon.

"Good to see you both," Officer Harrison's voice was calm, a contrast to the storm's erratic symphony. "Let's get you to safety."

His instructions were clear, simple, and Maddie found comfort in their straightforwardness. She followed him, her strides matching his, Dex at her side. The officer led them through the clearing, his back a shield from the biting wind that sought to claim every inch of warmth they had left.

"Almost there," he assured them, and Maddie clung to those words like a lifeline.

A blanket of silence enveloped them as they walked, the world reduced to the crunch of snow beneath their boots and the steady rhythm of their breathing. The clearing, once a sliver of hope, now expanded into a sanctuary as they drew nearer to the edge where safety awaited.

"Thank you," Dex managed to say, his tone infused with genuine gratitude.

"Doing my job," Officer Harrison replied, but there was a hint of warmth there, a shared understanding that they had weathered something monumental together.

Maddie glanced over at Dex, noticing the pink flush of his cheeks against the stark landscape. Their ordeal had peeled layers away, revealing the raw edges of vulnerability and strength alike.

Maddie's boots crunched on the snow, each step now buoyed by hope as shapes began to resolve into familiar figures. The clearing was speckled with people, and two of them surged forward, their relief palpable even at a distance.

"Mom! Dad!" Maddie called out, her voice breaking through the stillness. Laura and John Sullivan broke into a run, their faces a canvas of worry transforming into joyous relief as they closed the gap between them.

Her mother reached her first, wrapping Maddie in arms that were both soft and unyielding. Laura's tears spilled over, warm drops that cut through the cold on Maddie's cheeks. "We've got you," she whispered, her words a soothing balm.

John followed, his embrace encircling them both, his strength a fortress against the lingering chill. Their family unit, once fractured by uncertainty, was whole again. Maddie breathed them in, the scent of home mingling with pine and snow.

Nearby, Dex's laughter rang out, clear and bright as the thawing ice. Ava, no more than a wisp of a girl, clung to him—a fierce grip that belied her small stature. Her body shook, but Dex was there, his arms a safe haven against the tremors of fear and cold. "It's okay, Ava. I'm here," he soothed, his voice the lullaby of an older brother, a guardian.

In the clearing, amidst the huddle of families stitching themselves back together, Maddie caught Dex's gaze. His smile, a silent promise of shared secrets and quiet strength, warmed her more than any blanket could. They had walked through a storm, not just of snow and wind, but of their own fears and hopes. And they had emerged, not unscathed, but stronger for it.

"Let's go home," John said, his voice steady as the ground beneath the melting snow.

"Home," Maddie echoed, the word a sweet note in the symphony of their reunion.

Chapter Nine

Maddie's alarm pierced the calm of her room, a shrill herald to the start of school from winter break. She lay in bed for a moment, tangled in sheets that clung like remnants of the mountain mist, before finally swinging her feet onto the cool hardwood floor. The thrill of seeing her classmates again buzzed within her, yet it warred with a knot of nerves – an echo of the intense days spent with Dex, so close to danger and yet so alive.

She dressed in her usual practical style, choosing comfort over fashion, but today the fabric seemed to scratch at her skin, a reminder that she was heading back to a world where everything had changed, even if nobody else knew it.

As Maddie laced up her hiking boots – a silent nod to the mountains – there was a soft knock on the door. Brooke burst into the room, a whirlwind of curls and exuberance. Her hazel eyes scanned Maddie, searching for any sign of the ordeal she'd faced.

"Madison, you're okay!" Brooke enveloped her in a hug that smelled of strawberries and sunshine, a stark contrast to the earthy scent of pine that still lingered in Maddie's memory.

"Of course, Brookie," Maddie managed, her voice steady despite the storm of recollections Brooke's presence summoned. They settled on the edge of Maddie's bed, surrounded by walls adorned with maps and posters of distant horizons.

"Tell me everything," Brooke said, her voice bubbling with the kind of enthusiasm that made mundanity sparkle. "I missed you like crazy!"

"Let's just say it was an adventure," Maddie replied, the words catching slightly as she pictured Dex's easy smile in the glow of a cabin fire. "But I'm glad to be back."

Maddie and Brooke chatted about their summers, giggling like fireflies flitting around at night. For a moment, Maddie felt lighter, like she could almost forget her secret. Talking to her friend made her feel safe, like their friendship would help her navigate the unknown halls of Sequoia Grove High.

Maddie worried—She twirled her hair, something she always did when nervous. Brooke's laugh echoed in the air, a sound that usually cheered Maddie up. But today, it just reminded her of the big secret she had about Dex and the mountains. It felt so important, almost like another heart beating inside her.

"Brookie," Maddie started, her voice a hesitant whisper, "there's something I haven't told you about the trip."

Brooke tilted her head, her smile fading into a look of concern that creased her smooth forehead. "What's up? You can tell me anything, you know that."

The words tumbled out of Maddie, each one heavier than the last. She recounted the storm that had forced them into the cabin, the way the wind had howled like a beast at the door, demanding entry. She spoke of the fear, the isolation, and then, with a careful breath, of Dex—his jokes that cut through the tension, his steady presence that made the shadows less daunting.

"Wait, back up," Brooke interceded, her eyebrows knitting together. "You're telling me you and Dex, Mr. All-American Jock, actually... connected?"

Maddie's cheeks flushed a soft rose hue, a physical testament to the truth she laid bare. "Yes, we did. It wasn't just the circumstances, Brookie. There was something *real*." Her voice wavered, betraying the uncertainty that laced her conviction.

Brooke leaned back, arms crossed as she processed this revelation. Maddie could almost see the gears turning in her best friend's head, disbelief vying with the desire to understand. Brooke had never seen Dex as anything more than the charming athlete, too carefree for someone like Maddie. The idea that their Maddie, pragmatic and cautious, could share something profound with him seemed to challenge the very laws of their universe.

"Okay, this is... wow," Brooke finally said, her skepticism hanging between them like a question mark. "I mean, it's Dex. He's cool and all, but you two are like night and day, Maddie."

Maddie perched on the edge of her bed, hands clasped together as if to hold in the story that was spilling out. "You should have seen it, Brooke. The cabin was so... rudimentary. Just wooden walls and a flickering candle on the table." She gestured with her fingers, mimicking the dance of light and shadow. "The candlelight threw these long, quivering shadows against the wall. And outside—outside the wind was always there, howling like it wanted to sweep us away."

Brooke's feet tapped unconsciously, a metronome to her thoughts. "Candlelight and howling winds don't make a romance, Maddie," she said, though her tone had softened.

"Maybe not," Maddie conceded, tucking a strand of hair behind her ear. "But there was warmth too. Not from the fireplace—the warmth came from... us. From Dex and me, huddled together, sharing stories to distract ourselves from the cold."

Brooke's skepticism showed cracks, her taps slowing. "Sharing stories?" she echoed, as though tasting the words. "And...?"

Maddie looked crossed, "And, what?"

"Did you have sex?"

"No!" Maddie exclaimed, slapping her shoulder. "I think we both knew it wasn't the right time."

Brooke flipped her hair back and shook her head. "I can't believe it, Mads. You were alone in a cabin, stranded with the hottest guy in school, and you didn't hook up with him?"

Maddie felt insulted. "Of all people, Brooke. You *know* me, I'm not THAT girl."

Brooke swallowed her fun, "Yes, I know you. And you know me well enough I'm just saying what everyone at school will be *thinking*."

"He likes me, Brooke," Maddie confessed. "He *respects* me."

Brooke bit down on her lower lip. "I like that he respects you. Not many guys do … and I love, love, *love* that you shared stories. What kinna stories?"

I absolutely LOVE my best friend!

"Stories of our childhoods, fears, dreams. It was like the storm outside carved out a space for us, a temporary world where it was just him and me." Maddie's voice climbed, infused with the vividness of her recollections. "I remember his laugh, the way it filled the room, warmer than any fire could be."

Brooke watched, caught in the pull of Maddie's narrative. She saw the earnestness in Maddie's eyes, the way they shimmered with unshed emotion—a reflection of the sincerity that Brooke herself was starting to feel.

"His laugh," Maddie continued, "it made the fear seem

smaller, and every time he smiled at me, I felt... I felt like I was exactly where I was meant to be."

"Oh, Mads," Brooke breathed out, her skepticism dissolving into the air, much like the flickers of doubt in her heart. Her best friend, *her* Madison, had found something unexpected, something potentially beautiful, amidst the wildness of the mountains. And now, seeing the passion that radiated from Maddie, Brooke couldn't help but wonder if perhaps love could indeed bloom in the most unlikely places.

Maddie twisted a strand of her hair, then let it snap back into place. She watched the pattern on the rug blur through her vision, her voice a mere whisper when she spoke again. "But what if it was all just... you know, because we were there, trapped together? An illusion spun from necessity?"

Brooke's heel tapped against the floor, a metronome to Maddie's doubts. "You mean, like, maybe everything felt amplified because of the whole survival thing?"

"Exactly." Maddie's fingers traced the hem of her sleeve, her movements betraying the turmoil within. "What if ... now that we're back, he realizes it was just the adrenaline, the fear? What if..." She swallowed hard, and for a moment, the walls of her bedroom seemed to close in around her.

"Madison," Brooke said softly, her skepticism receding like shadows at dawn. Her eyes lingered on Maddie's downturned face, seeing the raw vulnerability that lay bare. In the silence, Brooke recognized the profound effect that the mountain ordeal had etched into her friend's heart.

"Hey," Brooke reached out, gently tilting Maddie's chin upward. "Listen to me, okay? Whatever happens with Dex, I'm here for you." Her voice was firm, a lifeline thrown across the chasm of Maddie's fears.

The corners of Maddie's mouth twitched, an attempt at a smile that didn't quite reach her eyes. "I know, Brookie. It's just... scary, thinking about seeing him at school, not knowing where we stand."

Brooke's expression softened, and she pulled Maddie into a side hug. "Life's pretty good at throwing curveballs. But you've got this amazing heart, and whatever comes, you'll handle it. With or without Dex."

A beat passed, filled only by the distant hum of traffic outside. Maddie leaned into the embrace, drawing strength from Brooke's unwavering presence. She inhaled deeply, the scent of Brooke's strawberry shampoo mingling with the lingering traces of pine from her own hair—a reminder of the mountains, of Dex, of everything that had changed and everything that remained uncertain.

Together, they rose, their friendship a beacon against the tumult of teenage life. Maddie squared her shoulders, a newfound resolve taking root. No matter the outcome, no matter the path ahead, she wouldn't have to face it without Brooke by her side.

Maddie slung her backpack over one shoulder, the weight of it a familiar comfort against her spine. "Brooke, before we head out," she started, pausing to look at her friend, "I just want to say thanks. For listening, you know? It means the world."

"Hey, that's what I'm here for," Brooke replied, her grin as bright as the sun that now peeked through the curtains. She gave Maddie's shoulder a gentle nudge. "Plus, after all the drama in those mountains, high school feels like a piece of cake!"

"Or a whole bakery," Maddie added with a chuckle, her nerves dancing like leaves in a soft breeze. The mountain memories clung to her like morning dew, fresh but fleeting.

"Come on, let's not be late for the grand entrance!"

Sequoia Grove High

Madison and Brooke walked side by side toward the school entrance.

"Madison Sullivan," Brooke began, her tone a blend of affection and gravity, "you've got me, now and always. Mountains, school hallways, whatever comes."

Maddie's throat tightened, her eyes glistening with unshed tears. The bond they shared was more than just years of laughter and whispered secrets; it was the knowing that when the world turned upside down, they had an anchor in each other.

"Thanks, Brooke," Maddie said, her voice a soft whisper battling the storm of emotions within. "I don't know how I'd do this without you."

"Hey, no heroics needed," Brooke replied, a playful twinkle in her eye. "Just two girls taking on the world, one day at a time."

The conversation shifted like autumn leaves in a gentle breeze, turning toward the looming halls of Sequoia Grove High. They spoke of teachers and textbooks, of pop quizzes that lay in ambush and essays that demanded late-night sieges.

"We'll tackle it together, Mad," Brooke said with determined cheer. "Study sessions at my place, yours, or even that old library if we're feeling adventurous."

"Adventurous? Is that what we're calling AP Biology?" Maddie quipped, the corners of her mouth inching upward.

"Absolutely. It's a jungle in there," Brooke laughed, her curls bouncing with the movement.

"Whatever happens with Dex," Maddie confided, "I won't let it wreck me. You and I, we've survived worse than awkward encounters by lockers."

"True." Brooke nodded sagely. "Remember seventh grade? The Great Glitter Incident?"

"Ugh, don't remind me," Maddie groaned, but the shared memory coaxed a genuine laugh from her, bright and clear as the lake at their beloved campground.

"See? Unstoppable," Brooke declared, squeezing Maddie's hand once more.

"Unstoppable," Maddie echoed, the word a promise, a

battle cry, a whisper of hope amidst the chaos of growing up.

Their laughter mingled with the morning air, a harmonious prelude to the symphony of high school corridors and classroom dramas awaiting them. Together, they would face it all—side by side, unfaltering, their friendship the steadfast compass guiding them through every challenge.

A ripple of laughter escaped them as they walked side by side, the bond between them an invisible thread stronger than steel. They moved with the confidence of warriors stepping into the fray, their friendship a shield against the slings and arrows of adolescence.

"Sequoia Grove High won't know what hit it," Maddie mused, her tone laced with playful bravado.

"Exactly," Brooke affirmed, her hazel eyes sparkling with mischief. "We'll conquer it together—like all those group projects we somehow aced."

"Except this time, no glitter explosions," Maddie quipped, remembering past misadventures with a shake of her head.

"Promise," Brooke laughed, crossing her heart.

Chapter Ten

Maddie's sneakers scuffed the sun-warmed concrete as she and Brooke melded into the throng of high school life at Sequoia Grove. Laughter and the clatter of locker doors punctuated the air, a symphony of teenage routine playing its familiar tune. Maddie let her gaze wander over the sea of heads bobbing through the corridors, searching.

"Any luck?" Brooke's voice was a buoy in the current of bodies, bright and expectant.

"Nothing yet," Maddie replied, her words clipped with the beat of her quickening pulse. Her eyes darted from face to face, each one not belonging to Dex adding weight to her anticipation. She could almost feel her heartbeat in her throat, a drumroll before the reveal.

"Keep looking," Brooke urged, her hand brushing against Maddie's arm in solidarity. Maddie nodded, grateful for the touch that grounded her to the moment.

Maddie had texted him the night before, but Dex seemed preoccupied, bothered for some reason. *Had she misread him? Maybe it was just the fear of being stranded in the snowstorm.* It was like trying to find a particular star on a cloudless night. Maddie knew Dex was there, somewhere; his presence was like an invisible string tugging at her senses. The crowd shifted, and for a brief second, a gap appeared, offering a fleeting hope, but it closed just as swiftly, taking the promise of his tousled blonde hair and mischievous blue eyes with it.

"Deep breaths, Madison," Brooke whispered, somehow sensing the crescendo of Maddie's internal symphony.

"Right," Maddie exhaled, watching her breath mingle with the early morning chill that lingered in the halls. She tucked a strand of brown hair behind her ear, willing her heart to quiet its frantic dance. In this ocean of students, Dex was her lighthouse, and all she needed was a glimpse to steer her wayward hopes back to shore.

The corridors of Sequoia Grove High swallowed Maddie's hope with each step she took, the sea of students parting around her and Brooke like ripples in a pond.

No Dex.

Her heart, once hammering in anticipation, now sank into an abyss of disappointment. The cacophony of locker doors and laughter sounded hollow, as if underwater.

"Maybe he's just late?" Brooke offered, her voice a buoy in the murky waters of Maddie's thoughts.

Maddie shook her head, her hazel eyes dimming. "No, he's always here by now." The words hung between them, heavy with unspoken fears. She felt the sting of tears threatening to breach her carefully constructed dam of composure.

"Hey," Brooke said softly, reaching out to tuck a rogue curl behind Maddie's ear, her touch gentle but firm. "Don't dive into that whirlpool. Dex... he's not worth drowning over."

But doubt was a relentless tide. Had his smiles been nothing more than distractions? Was it truly fear that had driven him to hold her hand, or something real?

"Brookie, what if..." Maddie's voice trailed off, her usual pragmatism dissolving into a pool of heartbreak. "What if all those moments meant nothing to him?"

"Then he's missing out on someone amazing," Brooke said, her tone threaded with conviction. "You're the girl who climbs mountains and laughs in the face of storms. Don't forget that."

Maddie's sneakers whispered against the linoleum, a soft counterpoint to Brooke's more determined tread. They moved through the throng of Sequoia Grove High students like twin rivers converging, each step an unspoken pact of solidarity. Maddie drew in a breath, trying to inflate her sagging spirits with the sterile scent of floor wax and textbooks.

"Remember," Brooke said, squeezing Maddie's shoulder gently, "you're Maddie Sullivan. You eat challenges for breakfast."

A chuckle tumbled out of Maddie, brief but genuine. "With a side of wild berries," she quipped, recalling the tangy sweetness of their campsite mornings. The memory was a life raft she clung to amidst the turbulent sea of high school hallways.

"Exactly." Brooke's grin was infectious, a bright spot in the beige expanse of lockers and classroom doors.

As they neared Maddie's locker, the hum of voices rose above the normal din. A knot of students clustered there, heads bobbing with curiosity. Maddie's pace faltered, her heart stuttering a strange rhythm. Brooke's eyebrows knitted together in confusion as they edged closer, peering over shoulders to glimpse the cause of the commotion.

"Is it a fight?" Brooke murmured, craning her neck.

"Or maybe someone's sick," Maddie suggested, but her voice was thin, laced with a thread of hope that something—anything—might be different today.

In the tangle of bodies, a splash of color snagged Maddie's gaze. Her feet rooted to the spot, and her pulse hitched at the sight of her once plain locker now festooned with balloons—ribbons of reds, blues, and greens dancing like leaves in an unseen wind. Nestled among them, half a dozen pink roses blushed a secret confession.

"Wow, impressive," Brooke's voice barely brushed Maddie's ear, a whisper lost in the sea of murmurs.

A romantic gesture so public, so unexpected, it snared Maddie's breath in her chest. She was pragmatic, always anchoring her heart before it could drift into daydreams. Yet here, in the unforgiving fluorescence of high school, fantasy bloomed against steel and cold combination locks.

The crowd parted, a curtain drawing back to reveal a stage set for a different kind of drama. Through the break in the sea of students, Maddie's eyes latched onto Dex's. His deep blue gaze held an earnest plea, a silent call across the divide.

Seconds felt like hours. Maddie was confused but hopeful, all mixed up like a tangled mess. This boy, with his easy smile and shrug, was a mystery. *Did he leave those flowers at her locker? Why would he?*

The crowd bustled around them, people coming and going, but Maddie barely noticed. She was totally focused on Dex, almost like he was pulling her in with an invisible rope. She felt a bunch of things at once: a little nervous about the past, excited about what might happen next, and a deep longing she hadn't quite admitted to herself yet.

Maddie's heart hammered in her chest like a drum solo. When Brooke took her hand, it felt like a steady rock in a rushing river. Taking a deep breath, Maddie let her backpack fall to the floor with a soft thump. Her hands trembled slightly at her sides as she took a step forward. Every move felt huge, a drumbeat matching her racing heart. She wasn't sure what was about to happen, but she knew she had to find out.

Dex walked towards Maddie, closing the gap between them even though things felt awkward. He stopped right in front of her, the lights buzzing overhead. He cupped her face gently, a light touch that sent shivers down her spine. There was a spark between them, like electricity.

"Maddie," he said softly, his thumb brushing her cheek in a sweet way that calmed her worries.

Dex's hands lingered on her face, everything around them quieting down. He gently pulled her into a hug. It felt like all the time they spent apart in school was just leading up to this moment. Maddie wasn't sure what to think, but she felt a little hopeful.

His hug felt warm and safe, like coming home after a long trip. It melted away all her doubts. As they held each other close, Maddie listened to his heartbeat. It was a steady rhythm, calming her own.

In his arms, the hallway noise faded away. It felt like the world got quieter just for them. Then, Dex spoke softly, his words a whisper in her ear. "I looked for you."

THE END

Escape the Ordinary. Find Your Spark.

Get swept away with Journey to Crystal Lake, a thrilling YA romance in two parts!

Maddie's annual camping trip takes a dramatic turn when a blizzard tears through the mountains, separating her from her family. Lost and alone, she finds herself in a deserted cabin... with Dex, the infuriatingly handsome boy from school who secretly holds her heart.

Will they find their way back together, or will the storm ignite a bitterness even fiercer than the blizzard?

Dive into Journey to Crystal Lake.

Start your adventure today!

Ebook & Paperback

About Lia

Lia Lucas is an emerging author of Urban Fiction, Young Adult, and Contemporary Romance. She has a wide range of writing interests and is currently living an incognito digital lifestyle.

Ms. Lucas is part of the Ardent Artist Books family.

Lia has published several books.

Also by Lia

YOUNG•ADULT

Journey To Crystal Lake - Part One

Snowbound with the Boy Next Door - Part Two

18+ • Adult

Curves

She Was Going Home

www.ingramcontent.com/pod-product-compliance
Lightning Source LLC
Chambersburg PA
CBHW070531160726

48003CB00004B/1750